Walt Disney's

DONALD DUCK in

Where's Grandma?

GOLDEN PRESS • NEW YORK
Western Publishing Company, Inc., Racine, Wisconsin

Copyright © 1983 by Walt Disney Productions. All rights reserved. Printed in the U.S.A. No part of this book may be reproduced or copied in any form without written permission from the copyright owner. GOLDEN®, A LITTLE GOLDEN SNIFF IT™ BOOK, and GOLDEN PRESS® are trademarks of Western Publishing Company, Inc. The "Microfragrance"™ labels were supplied by 3M Company. Library of Congress Catalog Card Number: 82-80186 ISBN 0-307-13207-2/ISBN 0-307-63207-5 (lib. bdg.)   B C D E F G H I J

Donald Duck and his nephews Huey, Dewey, and
Louie were going to spend a day on Grandma Duck's
farm. Donald's car bumped up the lane and stopped
in front of Grandma's house.

"Grandma, we're here!" called Donald.

But Grandma did not answer. Nobody answered.

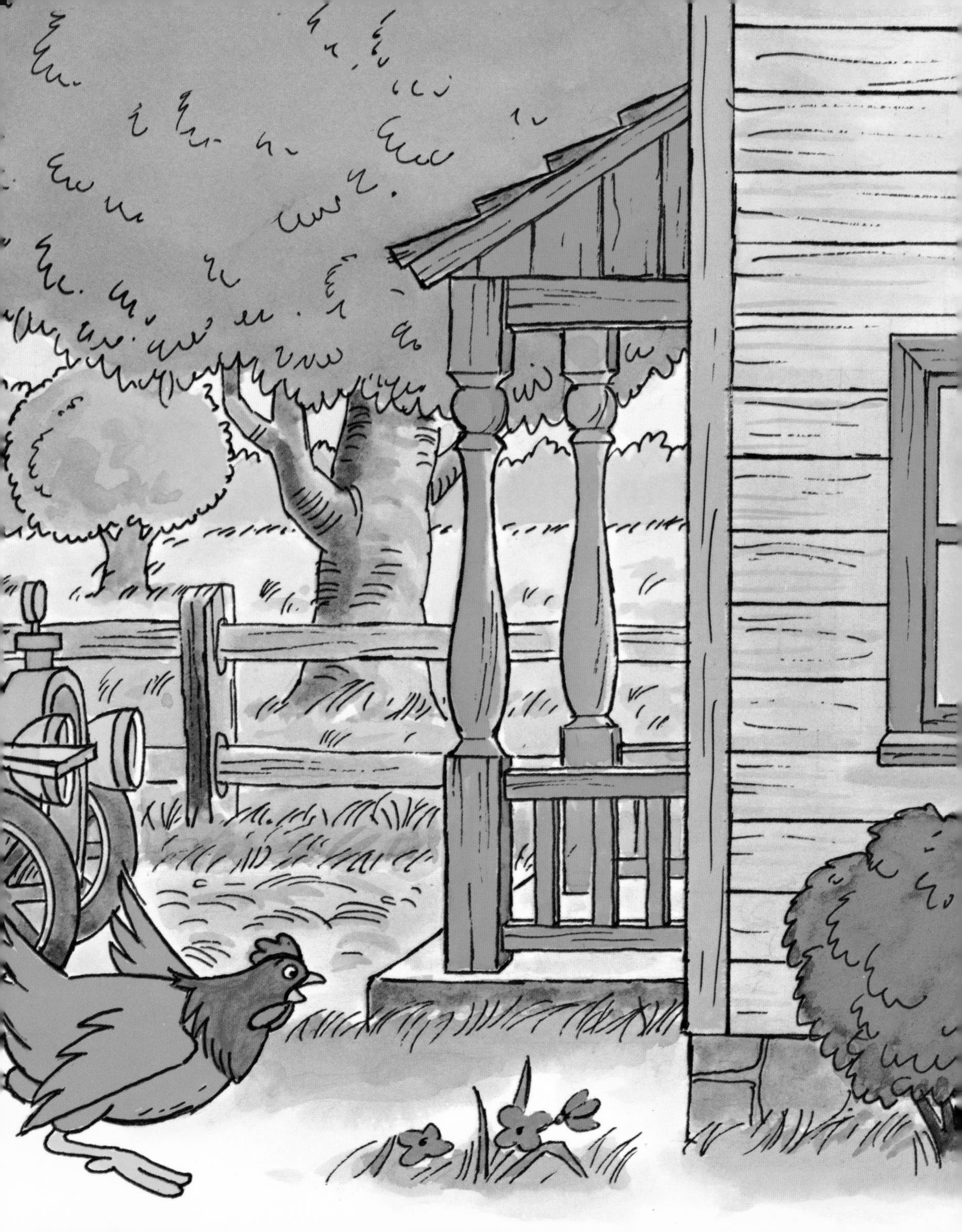

Louie opened the door to Grandma's kitchen. He
saw a big, frosty-cold pitcher of lemonade on the table
and a plate of cookies next to the pitcher. But he did
not see Grandma.

Huey looked in the springhouse. Cans of milk and crocks of butter stood in a corner. There was a sharp-smelling cheese on the shelf. But Grandma was not there.

Soon they came to the orchard. The air under the trees was cool and smelled like apples.

Then they saw Grandma and Gus Goose, perched in the branches.

"Watch out!" Grandma shouted. "The bull is loose!"

Donald turned
and saw the bull!
"Waaak!" yelled Donald.
He raced to the smokehouse
and darted inside.

The bull stamped and roared, but it couldn't get
at Donald. Finally it wandered away.

Donald was smudged and sooty when he came out
of the smokehouse. Grandma Duck had to march
him home and scrub him with yellow soap the way
she scrubbed him at bath time when he was little.

"There!" said Grandma, once Donald was wrapped in Gus Goose's big robe while waiting for his clothes to dry. "Now, would any of you boys like to pick some pumpkins?"

"We sure would!" shouted the nephews. They scooted out to the pumpkin patch and set to work.

They picked and picked. When they were through, Grandma baked the pumpkins into pies.

Then they sat down and had hot pie and milk. Huey, Dewey, and Louie each had two pieces of pie, but Donald had three.

"Being chased by a bull makes you extra hungry!" he declared happily.